T0333086

Ladybird  Readers

Peter and the Wolf

Series Editor: Sorrel Pitts
Text adapted by Coleen Degnan-Veness
Illustrated by Milly Teggle
Song lyrics by Pippa Mayfield

LADYBIRD BOOKS

UK | USA | Canada | Ireland | Australia
India | New Zealand | South Africa

Ladybird Books is part of the Penguin Random House group of companies
whose addresses can be found at global.penguinrandomhouse.com.
www.penguin.co.uk   www.puffin.co.uk   www.ladybird.co.uk

Penguin
Random House
UK

First published 2017
Updated version reprinted 2025
006

Copyright © Ladybird Books Ltd, 2017, 2025

Penguin Random House values and supports copyright. Copyright fuels creativity, encourages diverse voices,
promotes freedom of expression and supports a vibrant culture. Thank you for purchasing an authorized edition
of this book and for respecting intellectual property laws by not reproducing, scanning or distributing any part of it
by any means without permission. You are supporting authors and enabling Penguin Random House to continue to
publish books for everyone. No part of this book may be used or reproduced in any manner for the purpose of
training artificial intelligence technologies or systems. In accordance with Article 4(3) of the DSM Directive 2019/790,
Penguin Random House expressly reserves this work from the text and data mining exception.

Printed in Malaysia

The authorized representative in the EEA is Penguin Random House Ireland,
Morrison Chambers, 32 Nassau Street, Dublin D02 YH68

A CIP catalogue record for this book is available from the British Library

ISBN: 978-0-241-28434-6

All correspondence to:
Ladybird Books
Penguin Random House Children's
One Embassy Gardens, 8 Viaduct Gardens, London SW11 7BW

MIX
Paper | Supporting
responsible forestry
FSC® C018179

Ladybird Readers

Peter and the Wolf

Picture words

Grandfather

Peter

cat

wolf

little red bird

duck

meadow

pond

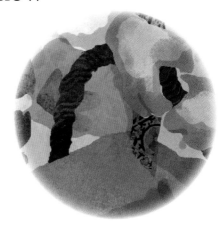

rope

Peter and his grandfather lived next to a beautiful meadow.

Next to the meadow, there was a dark forest. A hungry wolf lived in the middle of the forest.

"You must stay in the garden, Peter," said Grandfather. "Never go into the meadow alone."

"Why not?" said Peter.

"There is a hungry wolf in the dark forest," said Grandfather. "He will come into the meadow and eat you!"

Peter looked over the garden wall. The meadow looked very beautiful.

A little red bird flew up to a big tree. "Peter!" called the bird. "Would you like to come and play in the meadow?"

Peter climbed over the garden wall, and went into the meadow.

There was a pond in the middle of the meadow.

A duck walked past Peter. Then, she jumped into the pond, and swam away.

The little red bird flew down to
the duck.

"Come back!" she said to the duck.
"What a funny walk! Why don't
you fly like me?"

"I don't want to fly like you," said
the duck. "Why don't you swim
like me?"

The bird and the duck were very angry, and they made a lot of noise.

Suddenly, Peter saw a cat coming, slowly and quietly. It was preparing to jump on the bird and the duck.

"Careful!" called Peter. "The cat is going to catch you!"

At once, the little red bird
flew up to the top of the big
tree and the duck swam to
the middle of the pond.

At that moment, Peter's grandfather came into the garden.

He looked over the wall, and saw Peter in the meadow. He was very angry with him.

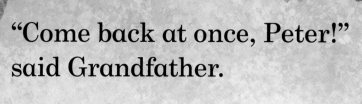

"Come back at once, Peter!"
said Grandfather.

So, Peter climbed over the wall,
and went back into the garden
with his grandfather.

Just then, the wolf came slowly and quietly out of the forest.

He saw the little red bird, the duck, and the cat. He was very hungry, and he wanted to eat them all.

The cat climbed to the very top of the tree, and waited with the little red bird.

"What's going to happen?" the bird asked the cat.

The frightened duck jumped out of the pond! She hurried away as fast as she could. But the hungry wolf ran faster, and he caught her in his big mouth!

Then, the wolf walked around and around the tree where the cat and the little red bird were sitting.

The hungry wolf looked up at them. They were very frightened.

Peter found a very long rope
and climbed on top of the
garden wall.

"Fly around the wolf's head!"
he called to the little red bird.
"Make his head go
around and around!
But don't go near
his big mouth!"

The little red bird flew above the wolf's head. The hungry wolf tried to catch the little red bird, but his head was going around and around. Soon, he fell down!

Peter climbed up the big tree. Then, slowly and quietly, he dropped the rope and caught the wolf's tail. The wolf jumped up and down, and tried to get away. But Peter held on to the rope.

At that moment, Grandfather saw Peter sitting in the tree.

"What are you doing up there?" he called.

"I've got the wolf," said Peter. "Look!"

Suddenly, two men came into
the meadow. "We're looking for
the wolf," they said.

"Here he is," said Peter.
"Take him away!"

The two men took the wolf to another forest, far away from Peter and his grandfather, the cat, and the little red bird.

43

"Peter, now you can play safely in the meadow with the little red bird and the cat," said Grandfather.

Everyone was happy.

Activities

The key below describes the skills practiced in each activity.

🖊 Spelling and writing

📖 Reading

💬 Speaking

🎧 Listening*

❓ Critical thinking

🎵 Singing*

✴ Preparation for the Cambridge Young Learners exams

*To complete these activities, listen to the audio downloads available at www.ladybirdeducation.co.uk

1 Look and read. Choose the correct words and write them on the lines. 📖 ✏️ ✴️

| Peter   Grandfather   wolf   meadow |

1 This is the name of the boy in the story.   _Peter_

2 This hungry animal lives in the middle of the dark forest.   ....

3 This person lives with his grandson, Peter.   ....

4 This is a beautiful place with grass and flowers.   ....

2 Circle the correct sentences.

1
a Peter lived with his grandfather.
b Peter lived with his cat.

2
a A little red bird lived in the forest.
b A hungry wolf lived in the forest.

3
a "You must stay in the garden!"
b "You must stay in the meadow!"

4
a Peter looked over the garden pond.
b Peter looked over the garden wall.

3 Match the two parts of the
sentences. Then, write them
on the lines. 📖 ✏️

1 Peter looked   **a** flew up to a
over the   big tree.

2 A little red bird   **b** garden wall.

3 "Peter!" called   **c** the bird.

1 Peter looked over the
garden wall.

2

3

4 Read the story.
Choose the right words and write them on the lines. 📖 ✏️ ✦

1 under	above	over
2 on	in	to
3 her	them	you
4 swim	swam	swimming

Peter climbed [1] .... over .... the

garden wall, and went into the meadow.

There was a pond [2] .... the

middle. It was beautiful. A duck walked

past Peter. Peter watched [3] ....

Then, she jumped into the pond, and

[4] .... away.

5 **Read the questions.**
Write complete answers.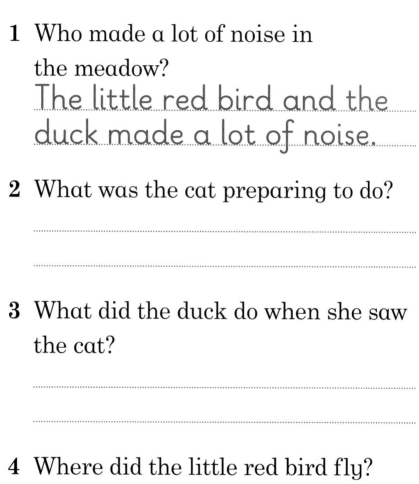

1 Who made a lot of noise in the meadow?

The little red bird and the duck made a lot of noise.

2 What was the cat preparing to do?

3 What did the duck do when she saw the cat?

4 Where did the little red bird fly?

6 **Look at the letters.**
Write the words.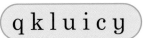

> q k l u i c y

1 The duck jumped .... *quickly* .... into
the pond.

> S n u d l d y e

2 ...., Peter saw a
cat coming.

> l y l o s w

3 The cat was walking ....

> t q u l i e y

4 The cat did not make a noise.
It walked very ....

> s l a f y e

5 The little red bird sat ....
at the top of the big tree.

52

7 Read the answers.
Write the questions.

1 Why did Peter have to stay in the garden?

Because there was a wolf in the forest.

2 Why _____

_____?

Because the little red bird wanted him to play.

3 How _____

_____?

He felt very angry with Peter.

4 Where _____?

Peter went back into the garden.

8 **Circle the correct words.**

1 The wolf came out of the
  a meadow.   **b** forest.

2 The wolf walked slowly and
  a quickly.   **b** quietly.

3 The wolf saw the duck in the
  a grass.   **b** pond.

4 The wolf was very
  a hungry.   **b** angry.

9 Ask and answer the questions with a friend. 🗨 ⬡

1 *Which animals did the cat want to catch?*

The little red bird and the duck.

2 Which animals did the wolf want to catch?

3 Which animal did the wolf catch?

4 How did the cat and the little red bird feel?

10 Write *to*, *in*, *up*, or *out*.

1 The cat climbed ....to.......... the very top of the tree.

2 The frightened duck jumped .... of the pond.

3 The hungry wolf caught her .... his big mouth!

4 The cat and the little red bird were sitting .... the tree.

5 The wolf looked .... at them.

11 Listen, and write the answers.

1 Who says this?

Grandfather

2 Who does the little red bird fly to?

3 Who says this?

4 Who is this?

5 What was going around and around?

12 Do the crossword.

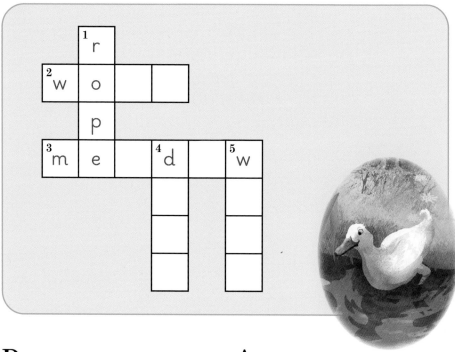

Down

1 Peter used this to catch the wolf.

4 This swam to the middle of the pond.

5 Peter climbed over this.

Across

2 This animal wanted to eat the duck, the little red bird, and the cat.

3 This is a beautiful place with trees and grass.

13 Talk about the two pictures with a friend. How are they different?

a

b

In picture a, Peter is on the wall, but in picture b, Peter is in the tree.

14 Who said this? 📖 ✏️

Grandfather Peter little red bird duck

1 "Never go into the meadow alone,"

said .... Grandfather ....

2 "What a funny walk!"

said the ....

3 "I don't want to fly like you,"

said the ....

4 "Fly around the wolf's head!"

said ....

5 "Take him away!"

said ....

15 Ask and answer the questions with a friend. 🗩 🗨

1

> Do you live in the countryside, a small town, or a big city?

> I live in a small town.

2 Who do you live with?

3 Are there any animals near your home?

4 Would you like to live next to a meadow? Why? / Why not?

16 **Listen, and** ✓ **the boxes.** 🎧 ⭐

1 Where is Peter?

a

b

c  ✓

2 What is Peter holding?

a

b

c

3 Which picture is it?

a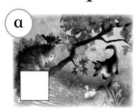

b

c

4 What is the bird doing?

a

b

c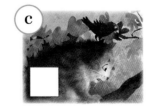

17 Sing the song.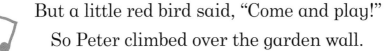

Don't go into the meadow. There's a hungry, hungry wolf.
But a little red bird said, "Come and play!"
So Peter climbed over the garden wall.
He went to play in the meadow
with the little red bird and the duck.

The bird and the duck talked noisily.
"Why don't you fly?" "Why don't you swim?"
And Peter saw a cat coming quietly to catch
the little red bird and the duck.

The little red bird flew into a tree,
and the duck swam into the pond.
Suddenly, a wolf came quietly to catch
the bird, the duck, and the cat.

The frightened duck jumped out of the pond,
and the hungry wolf soon caught her.
He came back to the tree and walked around,
looking at the bird and the cat.

"Fly around his head!" Peter said,
and soon the wolf fell down.
Peter caught the wolf with a rope on his tail.
And he didn't get the bird or the cat!
Now you can play in the meadow.
They've taken the wolf away.

Visit **www.ladybirdeducation.co.uk**

for more FREE Ladybird Readers resources

✓ Digital edition
   of every title

✓ Audio tracks (US/UK)

✓ Answer keys

✓ Lesson plans

✓ Role-plays

✓ Classroom
   display material

✓ Flashcards

✓ User guides

Register and sign up to the newsletter to receive your
FREE classroom resource pack!